FAT WIFE Loving HUSBAND

J. Postell

FAT WIFE LOVING HUSBAND

Copyright © 2022 by J. Postell

All rights reserved. No part of this book may be reproduced in any form or by any means, electronic or mechanical, including photocopying, recording, or by any information storage and retrieval systems, without permission in writing from the author, except where permitted by law and for reviews.

ISBN 978-0-578-38204-3

Printed in the USA
Published by SIP Publications, LLC & Junior Authors
Cover Design by 5:13 Graphics & Media, LLC
sisterspartnership@gmail.com
www.thejuniorauthors.com

Matthew

I recall the feelings I felt when I realized you were the one. A feeling of relief rushed over me. Never had I felt as safe, loved, and accepted. I could finally rest from all the games. I cried at the end of every date and not once did you judge me. I cried because this was it. You were the one and we both knew it. I didn't have to be anything but, me. My heart was finally safe.

Thanks for loving me!

Contents

65lbs of Baby FAT	1
Confident One Minute...	6
FAT & Fatherless	11
The FAT Mindset	18
Too Much FUPA in the Pants	24
Welcome to the...	29
The Skinny Wife	34
Stop Bringing Me...	39
He Loves My Short Hair	44
He Married a FAT Girl...	50
Yes, He's In Love...	55

This book is filled with facts about my life and my opinions fill every page. This book is not however the opinion, experience, feelings, or belief of every full-figured woman. This is my truth, marriage, and journey to deliverance.

Husbands, love your wives, *just as* **Christ also loved** *the church and gave Himself for her,* [26] *that He might sanctify and cleanse her with the washing of water by the word,* [27] *that He might present her to Himself a glorious church, not having spot or wrinkle or any such thing, but that she should be holy and without blemish.* [28] *So* **husbands** *ought* **to love their own wives** *as their own bodies; he who* **loves his wife loves himself.**

Ephesians 5:22-28

Dear Big Beautiful Wife

Being a wife, mother, leader, and Boss Chick is hard, but you're doing it! If you're like me, nobody sat you down and taught you how to be a wife. There's not a major in school that prepares us for this thing but somehow you are still crushing it!

The world told me what beauty was and I tried my best to ignore it. I wanted to set my own standard of beauty. I fight every day to hold up that standard. I check my heart just as much as I do my makeup. I fix my character just as much as I fix my hair.

We are all a work in progress, but while on the journey, I want you to remember this. You are fearfully and wonderfully made. You are in a league of your own and in competition with no one.

Your husband is blessed to have you and your family is favored because of you. Your daughter will grow up and want to be just like you and your son will pray that his future wife has some of your greatest qualities. You are amazing!

Your thighs may rub, your back fat may sweat, and you might get winded when chasing your dreams, but keep running, sis. Those that mock you will one day serve you and those that honor you will be exalted because of it.

Stay the course and never forget your worth…priceless!

Dear Brother

To the brother that has truly loved, honored, cherished and respected the full-figured woman in your life, I salute you.

To the brother that has caressed the thighs, kissed the belly and massaged the rolls of a big girl, I appreciate you.

To the brother that has openly applauded, loved and flaunted the big beautiful big chick on your strong masculine arm, I am proud of you.

It is not easy to be different, an independent thinker, a leader, but you Sir are doing it and we love you for it!

You are appreciated!!!

Introduction

Please do not let the title of this book fool you. I am a very confident woman. I am cute, fun, witty, anointed, intelligent, and multi-gifted. I never fish for compliments because I get them freely. Like most people, however, I have insecure moments. There are things about me that I would change and others that I dare not trade. My biggest insecurity has always been about my weight.

I was told that I was cute for a big girl, I dressed nice for a big girl, I was very confident for a big girl. Like being cute, nicely dressed, or confident is rare for a larger woman. I ignored the stereotypes but deep down inside, my insecurities due to my weight were challenging my self-esteem.

I recall telling a friend what this book would be about. I told her that I would be honest and share the insecurities I face as a larger wife.

She looked at me strangely and said, "What insecurities? You are one of the most confident women I know."

Confidence is a funny thing. It is either real or fake, but it can't be both. Had I faked being confident this whole time? I honestly love myself and I absolutely adore the woman that I have become. I thank God for who I am and what He's blessed me with daily. I am tired, however, of this life-like fat suit that holds the supermodel inside of me hostage. God help me get some darn self-control!

65lbs of Baby Weight

In a study of nearly 30,000 women who had given birth between one and four times, researchers found that most women never returned to their pre-pregnancy body weight after birth. Pregnancy can drastically change a woman's body and can lead to insecurities. The whole process of motherhood not only increases the feeling of doubt and insecurity in one's body and confidence but also in self-esteem.

I've always wanted a baby with my future husband. I imagined what we'd name him or her. If it were a boy, would he be mannish? Would he take after his strong father? Would she be sassy and no-nonsense like her mother?

The women in my family are very opinionated, loud, and strong. We also gain a lot of weight after having babies. Some gain more than others. After every birth, we are left with adorable babies and more "mommy weight" than one should be burdened with carrying.

The older you are, the harder it is to drop the baby

weight. That was especially true for me. I was 31 when I gave birth to my daughter. The bounce-back never happened for me. I'm sure I would have lost some weight had I breastfed as so many suggested. I wanted to breastfeed, but my daughter treated my nipples like they were the devil. She would scream at the top of her new lungs whenever I reached to whip them out to feed her. She was starving and my feelings couldn't bear any more rejection.

Eventually, I gave in to the peace that a milk-filled bottle would bring. The sad truth is, I didn't want to breastfeed her because of all the wonderful benefits it offered her. I wanted her to breastfeed to help me shrink the large waist she helped me gain.

Gaining 65 pounds after giving birth can do major damage to a girl's self-esteem. My stomach got bigger and so did my husband's affections towards me. Not once did his face read, "ugh" when undressing me. Not once did his manhood refuse to rise when making love to his larger wife. His kisses remained warm and sincere. It was my affection that secretly changed. I worried about how my larger body would look during sex. Would every position be secretly critiqued by him?

My sexy, seductive bedroom eyes were less appealing peeking over the chubby cheeks that stood mountain-like around them. Nothing about this baby weight was sexy to me. Every outfit I chose, I would later second-guess after looking in the mirror.

When asked his opinion, my husband would either thumbs up or thumbs down the style. Every thumb down felt like a personal shot fired at my body.

Before marrying Matt, I had lost almost 80 pounds. I was proud of my hard work, and I'd often reward myself with a pair of new jeans that further complimented the work I put in. I felt great! Until I had our baby. Most of the weight I'd lost was back and the extra pounds made it hard to believe my husband when he said I was beautiful. I didn't feel beautiful. Cute definitely but calling me beautiful felt like a pity compliment given because he knew I had changed.

I used to hate it when people told full-figure women they had a pretty face. It's insulting, but there I stood in the mirror telling myself, "Well, at least you still have a pretty face." I had to get my confidence back and it was going to take more than my husband complimenting me to restore it. I had to find a way to love myself again, big or small.

Self-Reflection:

1. Is your self-esteem influenced mainly by your appearance?
2. If your appearance drastically changed, would you still love yourself?
3. Name at least 3 of your greatest qualities that aren't physical.
4. How do you determine your self-worth?

Confident One Minute and Insecure the Next

A 2014 survey conducted by Glamour magazine and Ohio State University confirmed that women have admitted to not feeling good about their bodies — regardless of their age or weight. Whether they are a size 6 or a size 20, they don't feel they add up to the picture-perfect women they are continually seeing in social media, TV, and magazines.

Explain to me how I could feel confident one minute and insecure the next? I honestly believe that confidence is something you feel at different moments, just like insecurity. One day, I could feel like a bad boss chick, ready to take over the world. The next day, I could feel completely discouraged because I couldn't find an outfit that complimented my body for date night.

How is every outfit I own suddenly wrong? I've been wearing these same clothes for years. If the clothes didn't change, then my body did. Whether I gained weight or not, I was determined to always represent my husband and big wives everywhere. You'd never get the chance to say that you saw me looking a mess, smelled me, or could see fat roll imprints through my clothes. I refused to be stereotyped by anyone. Stereotypes like, big women are lazy, desperate and have low self-esteem are simply untrue. Like most women we have insecurities but loving ourselves less, doesn't automatically come with the territory just because our bodies are larger.

I was completely confident in what my husband and I had built together, but my "**FAT** girl insecurities" would creep in from time-to-time making me feel unstable. I don't like having feelings of insecurity. Insecurity makes me feel weak and vulnerable. Two things I hate.

I was the first big girl my husband had been with. What did he know about back fat, FUPAs, and inner thighs rubbing? This man was a "newbie," and I was blessed to be the one to welcome him aboard but secretly, that scared me.

"You're so beautiful baby," he'd say.

I'd reply with a flirty, "Thanks, babe." Then, not even a minute later, I'd look in the mirror at my rosy cheeks and second guess every compliment he'd just given.

I vividly remember him staring at me one day.

"What?" I asked.

"You're so adorable baby," he replied.

I blushed on the outside portraying confidence, but I cringed on the inside. His compliment embarrassed me somehow. And why was he staring at me in the first place? On one hand, I agreed with him. Hell, I am adorable. But then, on the other hand, I wanted to know what made me so adorable to him?

I swear! This insecure chick was slowly trying to ruin my marriage!

Eventually, I had to talk to my husband about my insecurities. I explained how I was feeling about myself and the struggle to stay positive. I needed his encouragement regardless of how I was feeling about my body.

When you have a great relationship, you do what it takes to make it stay that way. You communicate even when it hurts. You get the help required even when you don't want it. My marriage was worth fighting for. I was worth fighting for. The insecure chick in my head was not going to ruin me. I was determined to be declared the overall winner.

Self-Reflection:

1. Have you or your spouse's insecurities affected your relationship in any way?
2. Do you know the signs of insecurity in a relationship?
3. Have you talked to your partner about your or their insecurities?
4. How do you deal with insecurities in your relationship?

FAT & Fatherless

"Fatherless Daughter Syndrome" (colloquially known as "daddy issues") is an emotional disorder that stems from issues with trust and lack of self-esteem that leads to a cycle of repeated dysfunctional decisions in relationships with men. It can last a woman's entire lifetime if the symptoms go unacknowledged and ignored.

I don't care what anyone says, a young girl needs her father. I denied that fact for years. I brushed it under the rug and hid it like I did those insecurities. I didn't need him just like he apparently didn't need me. My mother did her thing and he missed out, not me. I believed those words. I praised them, repeated them in my heart, and lived by them for years.

I wasn't like those girls that looked for their father in men. I wasn't trying to be with anything that emulated him in any way. I wanted better for my life.

I deserved better. I was raised by a strong single mother. Every moral, value, and piece of strength I had come from her, and her alone. This was an area in my life where my confidence shined. The only problem was I was wrong, and my father's absence affected me more than I knew.

When I met Matt, I instantly gave him the nickname, "My Matt." I didn't know why I'd chosen that name. I'd never called any other guy I dated "my" anything, so why now? He didn't belong to me. He wasn't my property. He wasn't even my man yet and there I was laying claim to him.

The Lord later revealed to me that I finally had a man in my life that loved me unconditionally. That is the role of a father. This was something I'd never experienced.

I finally had something that was "mine." He wanted me and I wanted him. He wasn't just a boyfriend, and my spirit knew it. This was more, this was divine.

Matt's love honestly felt different, which made me feel safe. He was loving and trustworthy and patient and those were all the qualities of a father. I finally had what I lied to myself and told myself I didn't need.

Unfortunately, this became a serious problem. If he didn't kiss me at the right time, I felt rejected. If he didn't hold my hand in public, I was secretly angry. When he did grab my hand or show PDA it made me feel uncomfortable.

"What is wrong with me?" I thought. The real issue lied in my upbringing. I wasn't raised by both parents and the absence of my father left me with a major deficit. I was emotionally handicapped. My balance was off, and it forced my new husband to hold me up emotionally, or at least until I was ready to be healed. The only problem is you can't heal what you won't admit is broken.

I finally had to admit the truth. My father broke my heart. His absence left an indelible mark on my heart.

I needed him just as badly as I needed my mother. My husband was often left guessing what affection I needed because I wouldn't tell him. I wanted him to magically read my heart and mind. I know I didn't marry a mind reader, but I wanted him to have the ability from time-to-time.

A father proudly holds his little girl's hand. He does it because he loves her, and he wants to keep her safe. It's normal to her. She expects it from him and when he doesn't do it, without hesitation she will grab his.

Deep down inside, I wanted Matt to always reach for my hand. I wanted to reach for his, but it felt weird. I always wanted a loving husband like Matt, but nobody prepared me for him. Having a father would have prepared me for him. I would know how to receive love. I believe that natural things like holding hands wouldn't feel foreign to me had I been raised by a loving father.

I later learned to communicate these weird emotions.

He understood the complexity of my heart and he did what felt right to him. He simply loved me. Sometimes he forced me to hold his hand in public because that's what he needed. Our love slowly but surely became balanced, but it was going to take work that would unearth a side of me that I didn't even know existed.

Steps to Healing:

1. **Seek Help:** *You can't do this by yourself. Seeking professional help will bring you one step closer to the emotional and mental healing you deserve. You are not a victim; you are a victor. Getting the professional help that is required when experiencing this kind of pain will only make you stronger emotionally. Don't stop until you are whole.*

2. **Know Your Emotional Triggers:** *When you become aware of the emotional and behavioral impact of having an absent father, you can better choose how to respond to the hurt you experience. Healing comes when you can identify your emotional triggers and handle them wisely.*

3. **Look Internally:** *We need others, but we must put our relationship with ourselves first. Only then are we truly ready to attract someone with whom we experience genuine love.*

4. **Be Selective:** *Be selective with who you date, let in, and ultimately marry. Know your worth, guard your heart, and refuse to negotiate your boundaries. Be leery of those that want to rush "love." Choose someone who has healthy boundaries and who will take their time getting to know you. You deserve genuine love.*

5. **Forgive**: *Forgiveness is for you, not them. You deserve to be whole and that can't happen when you purposely hold on to pain. Forgiveness is hard but it is necessary to live a happy, healthy, whole life.*

Self-Reflection:

1. Did growing up with or without a father affect you in any way? If so, how?
2. Has being fatherless affected your romantic relationships?
3. Was your self-esteem affected due to growing up without a father? If so, how?
4. What help, if any, have you sought to deal with these issues?

The FAT Mindset

We can all define the word: FAT. You don't need Webster's help on that one. But what is a "Fat Mindset?" I believe a "Fat Mindset" is a stumbling block in the mind that keeps you from total freedom.

The "Fat Mindset" tells you things like...

-You're not good enough

-You'll never truly be happy

-You'd be perfect if...

-Your sexiness has boundaries

-Your beauty has boundaries

The "Fat Mindset" is like cancer to your self-esteem and it is killing you slowly. My husband always says one of the sexiest things about me is my confidence. Ironic, huh? The truth is: I am confident most days.

Give me a mic, a stage, and a room full of energetic people and there's no stopping me. I make people laugh,

I inspire them, I give them hope. I make them feel welcomed and I never meet a stranger. Does that sound like a woman with insecurity issues?

Most people would never know I secretly struggle with insecurity because I don't introduce that side to them. The woman they meet is genuine, but there's more to her than the social butterfly that just worked the room.

Nobody gets to meet the insecure woman except Matt. Only he knows the woman that questions if I honestly look good in an outfit, if my fat rolls are visible or if my stomach is protruding in this shirt. You might not look at this as insecurity, but when you try on multiple outfits, or delete picture-after-picture because you look fat in that one, insecurity quickly becomes the culprit.

The "Fat Mindset" can certainly destroy an evening. For example, wearing supportive undergarments under that dress makes it look better on me. The "Fat Mindset," however, can make you believe that the undergarments barely hide anything and they'll still be able to see what you're trying to keep hidden. This then makes me feel self-conscious, which in turn makes me change. Years ago, if I couldn't find an outfit that "worked," I would cancel our evening altogether, further frustrating my husband.

The "Fat Mindset" can also make you believe that you must overcompensate for your size. I'm not into expensive name brands but I can put some pieces together. I am naturally stylish, but because I am a full-figure woman, I make sure to put extra care into my appearance.

I always want to represent myself and my husband well when we go out. When that doesn't happen, I am not happy. I can't just throw on a tank top, a pair of jeans, and some shoes and go. No, getting dressed for me is an entire production.

I have to put on my girdle, make sure my overly-large breasts are touching my chin which is why I only go to specialty shops when bra shopping. I have to throw on a blazer or blue, jean jacket over these arms because I refuse to show them in public. I hate seeing pictures of me and my arms or stomach look huge. This plays over and over in my head when going out, so I have to make sure the undergarments I wear help eliminate that fear.

I critique and judge everything about myself at that moment. I compliment myself on what's right, but that can easily become overshadowed by the things that are wrong. All big women are not created equal. This is why the "Fat Mindset" is not an issue that only larger women have. You can be a size 5 and have body image issues. Insecurity comes in all shapes, shades, sex, and sizes. It does not discriminate.

Now, I won't blame every insecurity I have on the size of my waist, but when the scale tips past a certain point or when the way you think you look in a certain outfit doesn't match the reflection in the mirror, insecurities associated with your weight will soon follow.

My insecurities surrounding my size have honestly become less and less. My husband's love and support have contributed to that, but I had to do the work. Slowly but surely, I'm getting better. If I like an outfit, I wear it. I look in the mirror once and keep it moving. I refuse to obsess over every little thing. I remind myself of my worth and walk like the big, bad chick that I am. I can't depend on anyone to make me feel good about myself. That's my job and I won't quit!

Self-Reflection:

1. Has toxic thinking affected your relationship? If so, how?
2. Did you know that overthinking is rooted in insecurity? How has overthinking affected your relationship?
3. Is there something that you're afraid of that may be impacting your negative thinking?
4. How do you cope with your insecurities?

Too Much FUPA in the Pants

I recall hearing a woman say that looking good in her clothes motivates her to stay committed to going to the gym. Looking good in my clothes motivates me to go to the gym, too. It's just not enough to make me stay committed. I've tried and I've succeeded. I've lost weight and gained it back at least twice. Recently, nothing has been able to make me stay consistent until I put on my favorite jeans and couldn't button them.

There's nothing worse than looking like you've stuffed yourself into your clothes. Fitted and tight are two very different things. I couldn't believe it. Had I gained that much weight since last summer? I finally got them buttoned but this time, my girdle didn't help hide the overflow that spilled out on top of my jeans. I looked and felt like a carefully stuffed sausage.

I openly expressed my frustration to my husband. I told him that I was tired of my FUPA, and I wanted to look good in everything I put on. I informed him of what I was and was not allowed to eat. I was going back to the gym, and I wanted him to help hold me accountable. What I forgot was that you can't tell Matt to hold you accountable and not expect him to do so.

The first few weeks I did great. I went to the gym and I stopped eating sweets. I had become consistent. I was committed. On the days that I didn't go to the gym, Matt would gently hold me accountable by asking, "Are you going to the gym today, baby?" Suddenly I became enraged! I mean, was he Billy Blanks, now? Did I hire him to coach me without my knowledge? Who paid him because I surely didn't!

"Yes, Matt! I'm going!" I responded, with a death stare and an intense eye roll. I grabbed my keys and stormed out of the stupid house! I honestly hated him at that moment. He didn't know anything about what I was going through. He could just stop eating sweets for two weeks and lose 8 pounds. I stopped eating sweets for two whole months and gained 2 pounds! He didn't understand this struggle. He has never struggled with his weight. Suddenly, after 12 years of marriage, he has a little belly and he thinks we're the same. How dare he ask me if I were going to the gym!

Why was I so angry at him? He was only doing what I asked him to do. I taught healthy relationship classes for years and I knew that I needed to attack the problem and not Matt. Once I calmed down and thought about my reaction to his gentle accountability, I knew I was wrong. Reminding me to go to the gym felt like rejection. He asked if I were going to the gym, but I heard, "You're fat and you need to go to the gym."

Once again, insecurity had reared its ugly head and convinced me that Matt hated having a fat wife. I knew the truth, but the lie seemed easier to believe.

I mean, why would anyone be okay with being married

to a bigger woman when they could have a smaller one? Even writing this question breaks my heart. Why did I feel less deserving of his love because of my size? Do larger women not deserve love? Of course, we do. We are humans capable of love and deserving of love.

Sharing my insecurity with others hurts. You only want people to see the best in you, but I believe that true authenticity is what brings about real deliverance. I couldn't let my insecurities rob me of the help that I so desperately needed. I needed my husband to hold me accountable because doing so was love. Confessing your truth is the only way to kill the lie.

I still can't fit into my favorite jeans like I used to, but the spillage is gone. I'm taking it one day at a time. Soon my favorite jeans will be too big, and I will thank my husband for encouraging me to get healthy.

Self-Reflection:

1. Have you shared your insecurities with your partner?
2. Do you trust your partner enough to hold you accountable? Why or why not?
3. Does your partner hold you accountable? If so, how does that make you feel?
4. Do you hold your partner accountable? Why or why not?
5. Has your spouse encouraged you to get healthy in any way? Does it feel like love or judgment to you?
6. Do you feel deserving of love? Why or why not?

Welcome to the Amusement Park

Zava, conducted a survey that polled over 1,000 men and women about what made them feel uncomfortable in bed and how it hindered their enjoyment of sex. While men were more likely to be insecure about their performance, 79% of women reported body image to be their biggest insecurity.

Making love is without question one of my favorite things to do with and to my husband. I am confident in my ability to please him, and my generosity is appreciated and given back to me a hundredfold.

Insecurity had no place in our bedroom until the first time Matt folded me up like a cheap toddler mattress. In between each passion-filled thrust, I'd think to myself, "What does my stomach look like from his view?" I felt like a Little Debbie's Swiss Roll, but did I look like one, too?

Insecurity never takes a day off, so you must be ready to kill it at any moment. Even during sex. The enemy will do anything to ruin the ministry of lovemaking with your spouse. He works overtime to sever marriages so using my weight and the insecurities that came with that was his goal.

I was fully aware of his diabolical plan, so I made it my mission to ignore the insecurities that tried to arise while making love. I will not be outwitted by the deceiver. The bible says that the marriage bed is undefiled, and I make sure to use that scripture to my full advantage.

I ignore the insecurities by working harder to please my husband sexually. I am sensual and I do positions that I know show off every inch of my curvy body. As my freedom grew so did my sexy acrobatic moves. Soon my round, gyrating belly became minuscule. Matt loved every part of me, and I knew it.

Studies have shown that body dissatisfaction can not only make it harder for women to get aroused, but it often means we'll avoid certain positions or acts we enjoy, purely out of insecurity. Body image insecurities hinder our sexual arousal, which then affects the whole sexual encounter.

Sex is one of the most intimate acts between a husband and wife. If you can't trust your spouse with your literal nakedness, then how can you trust him or her with your insecurities?

Women are sexually stimulated by what we hear. So, the more a man compliments, encourages and celebrates his wife, the more sex she wants to give. Feeling safe for women is closely tied to our desire to have sex with our partners.

Matt has always affirmed my beauty and dispelled my insecurities, which made sex a welcomed exchange. If I didn't feel safe, loved, or appreciated, then sex would feel more like a chore for both of us.

Instead of worrying about his view of my FUPA, I imagine my big, curvy body as his amusement park. The park is filled with loops, hoops, twists, and turns. It has coming attractions and it's filled with fun activities. He has been granted all-access-only passes and the park is never closed to him.

Self-Reflection:

1. Has a negative body image affected you and your partner intimately?
2. Would gaining or losing weight affect your sex life? Why or why not?
3. Does self-esteem affect your sex drive?

The Skinny Wife

Being confident 100% of the time is wonderful, it's just not realistic. Nobody likes to admit that they're insecure, afraid, or even intimidated- but here we are. I've learned a few things since being a big woman.

#1 Everybody loves either cake or pie

#2 Nobody's perfect

AND LASTLY

#3 **Smaller doesn't mean better!**

Sometimes the grass seems greener and healthier in the "yard" of the woman that wears a size 6. On the outside, she seems happy and healthy. She doesn't seem to lack determination or self-control. Her midnight hunger cravings don't show in her face nor on her waist. If she's married, you may even assume her spouse is happy. If she's single, then her dating life portrays an elaborate adventure, but I've learned to look closer.

Everybody has something they'd like to change

about themselves. It may not be the same as yours but none of us can escape humanity.

I recall meeting my husband's friend and his new wife. She was an average looking woman but she seemed extremely confident, well-dressed, and skinny. She also had the longest bundle of 1B Indian Remy hair I'd ever seen.

I'd checked her out from head to toe in 4 seconds flat. Throughout the night I found myself comparing little things about her to myself. We often compare ourselves to others because we admire something they have that we lack. The only thing she seemed to have that I lacked was the ability to fit into a size 5.

Her long hair made me question my short, natural cut. Yes, my hair is dope, but maybe I, too, would look like a pageant Queen if I tried wearing a long weave. She laughed at everything her husband said and he hung on her every word.

The two seemed to be made for each other in every way.

Theodore Roosevelt called comparisons the "thief of joy" and he was right. Nothing about what I was doing was bringing me any peace, but I couldn't stop myself. Nobody wants to play the "comparisons game" but those of us that have compared ourselves to other women understand the shame you feel immediately after. You don't want to do it. You hate doing it, but like an unwanted sneeze during a prolific speech, it happens.

Comparing can also be inspiring. It can make you work harder to meet your goals. But more times than not, it's detrimental to your self-esteem. Dwelling on the best part of someone's life and the worst of yours can be dangerous.

Blinders or Blinkers are leather or plastic cups placed on a horse's bridle or hood. The Blinders cover the rear vision of the horse, forcing it to look only in a forward direction and keep it on track.

I wanted desperately to enjoy this woman, so, I put on my metaphoric blinders and gained a new friend.

What I later learned after getting to know her was that she was deeply insecure. She didn't trust her husband and she showed it by needing to be with him constantly.

What looked like best friends was an insecure wife and a sneaky husband. Her greatest fear was infidelity and a few short years later, her fears became her unfortunate reality. He was a dog and his doggish ways were started to affect and infect his marriage, literally.

My comparisons didn't stop once I realized how insecure she was. They stopped when I realized how great I was. I focused on what I loved about myself and rehearsed it out loud. It may sound crazy, but it works. I affirmed myself and little by little, in my mind, no one compared to me. Nobody can beat you being you. Toxic comparing, crushed!

Self-Reflection:

1. Do you compare yourself to others? Why or why not?
2. What things, if any, do you compare?
3. Do you know why making comparisons is toxic to your mental and emotional health?
4. How does comparing yourself or your life to others make you feel?
5. Why do you compare yourself to others?

Stop Bringing Me Candy!

Matt isn't the most romantic man, but he is extremely thoughtful, which is romantic to me. He doesn't surprise me with tickets to my favorite show, but if I mention being tired, he's dropping everything to make sure I rest. If I say my feet hurt, he'll stop what he's doing to come and rub them. This is the reason mentioning my favorite snacks in front of Matt is dangerous.

I love candy! It's one of the reasons I've had cavities and still have chunky thighs. My husband is fully aware of my addiction to Airheads, Reese's Peanut Butter Cups, and anything with chocolate. I often lack self-control when trying to refrain from eating sugary snacks, so, it's best that I stay away from them altogether.

He doesn't bring me home candy often, but when he does, I get very excited.

"Aww, babe this was so sweet, but you have to stop bringing me candy."

I say while politely snatching the tasty gift from his tight remorseful grip. I happily shake my thighs while enjoying the chocolaty goodness but in the back of my mind, I think to myself, "why did he bring me this?" I know he's not doing it to hurt me. Quite the opposite. He does small things like this because it's one of the ways he demonstrates love. He likes to make me happy, and he knows that candy makes me happy.

Matt knows my struggle with my weight, but if I'm not complaining about it or trying to change it, then Matt assumes I don't mind indulging in a treat. His thoughtfulness is very much appreciated. I wouldn't appreciate a bag of apples like I would a piece of cake, although the apples are what I need.

Yes, he surprises me with candy from time-to-time, but he's also the reason we take such good care of our immune and digestive systems. One of my favorite teas he makes for us has ginger root, lemon, turmeric,

Burdock root, and agave for a touch of sweetness in it.

Matt didn't know that he had become a food enabler. He thought he was simply making his wife happy. Being strong and communicating that I need him to help me resist these sorts of snacks was hard, but necessary.

I'd be lying if I told you he stopped buying sweet treats. He still brings snacks home periodically, but I'm learning how to resist the urge to indulge. The truth is, Matt isn't the one with the problem. He's working on being healthier. I recall bringing him home things that weren't the best for him. Unlike me, he can resist the urge to overindulge.

I am a work in progress, and I too am learning how to say no. It is important that we both communicate our boundaries to each other. I know that if I tell Matt to stop bringing me candy, he'll do that. I also know that if he knows I like something, he will have to fight the urge to get it for me. He isn't perfect, but like a sweet treat made with honey instead of sugar, he is my perfect balance.

Self-Reflection:

1. Is your spouse an enabler? If so, how?

2. Will he or she do anything to make sure you're happy?

3. Have you communicated your boundaries with your spouse?

4. Is there an area of your relationship that is unhealthy and in need of repair? Have you communicated this to your spouse?

He Loves My Short Hair

"Short hair is perceived as only being attractive on a woman who is slender and/or physically fit." Jo-Ellan Dimitrius cites findings from her survey of more than 1,500 Americans that shaped the book, *"Put Your Best Foot Forward: Make a Great Impression by Taking Control of How Others See You."*

I've had a thick head of hair all my life, so cutting it off was never a big deal to me. I love short, trendy hairstyles. One of my favorite things to do with my hair is to shave the sides. After leaving the barbershop I feel cute, edgy, and strong. I can't explain it. I've always enjoyed the results of going to the hairdresser but waiting had become brutal. When I go to the barbershop, I'm in and out in less than 30 minutes. Talk about empowering!

Most husbands would go crazy if their wife cut their hair- not mine. Before cutting my hair, I always show my husband the cut I'm considering. He's loved every style I've worn. He also likes my short hair because he says it brings out my face.

Recently, I had been feeling down on myself because I hadn't been able to stick with my latest gym routine. I knew I needed to lose weight and was determined to do so. The only thing that was stopping me was my lack of willpower and determination.

My shaved sides and short natural cut that I once loved, along with my weight issues, started to make me feel somewhat unattractive. I realized I started to hate my short hair because I hated my weight. Maybe if I could lose the weight, I would love my short cut again.

Growing my hair back was the one thing I felt I could control at the time. I struggled with self-control so losing weight seemed impossible, but I could always grow hair and even if I couldn't, I could buy it. Weave is it's an instant self-esteem booster for a lot of women. If you can't grow it, you can sew it. Weave in my opinion is just another way to cover the imperfections for so many. It's like beautiful curtains hiding stained glass windows. You don't know how rare and beautiful the window is until you push back the curtains.

Weave, wigs and any other hair extensions are fine as long as you feel just as beautiful without it, as you do with it. Remember, hair is the accessory, not the main attraction. It takes real confidence to wear short natural hair. Confidence that I had until I didn't.

One of the things I love and hate about Matt is his honesty. When he came home, I looked him square in the eyes and said, "Do I look like a dude?"

Without hesitation and with a serious tone he said, "Are you crazy? Nothing about you resembles a man. You're beautiful."

Having a loving, supportive husband is important to a woman raised without a father. Every girl wants to feel beautiful, and her father reassures her of that. I love watching my husband father our daughter. Knowing that she has an earthly father that loves her unconditionally makes my heart smile. I don't know how God did it, but He knew that I needed a loving husband who would love our little girl, and in turn, that love would heal the little girl in me.

I lost a total of 5 whole pounds; my sides are still shaved and I'm loving it. Yes, I need to lose weight and yes, some days I feel average, but most days you can't tell me anything! My husband thinks I'm fine and that's all the reassuring I need. You'd be surprised what healing and unconditional love will do for your self-esteem. It also does wonders for your skin. My melanin stays glowing!

Listen, the Lord knows that I love my husband, but if he decides to leave today, eventually, I will be okay. If I gain all 5 of those pounds that I lost back, I will still be beautiful. My husband didn't heal my broken pieces. He simply showed me where they were. It is up to me to do the work required to put them back together again.

Self-Reflection:

1. Does hair affect your confidence?
2. Does a certain hairstyle boost your confidence?
3. Does your partner have an opinion on what you do or don't do to your hair?
4. How does your hair impact your self-esteem?
5. If you cut your hair, how do you think your partner would respond?

Ask yourself this question and be very honest...
Am I beautiful without hair and makeup? Why or why not?

He Married A FAT Girl - Part 1

Mind Reading (Toxic Thinking): *Assuming you know what other people are thinking. Your insecurity puts imaginary judgmental thoughts in other people's heads, which you then believe wholeheartedly, which in turn makes you feel more insecure. It's a vicious circle of epic proportions. Mind reading makes you think others are either judging or rejecting you.*

I often wonder what people think of Matt and I when they first meet us. If I didn't know us, I'd instantly love us. We're cool, nice, fly, approachable and genuine. Those are the nice thoughts that run through my head, but my next thought is, "What do they think of me?"

Now, to be fair, this thought is more narcissistic than it is insecure. And yes, most narcissists deep down inside are insecure, but what was my excuse? I'm not a narcissist.

I have narcissistic traits like most people, but it's never all about me. That is- until I think it is.

The "Fat Mindset" doesn't stop because you just will it to. You must confront this wrong thinking daily. If you fail to do so, you will constantly be bullied by these ruthless thoughts. Sometimes these negative thoughts creep in when Matt introduces me to someone for the first time. I wonder if they're thinking, "Oh…he's married to a fat girl." I know I'm projecting when I assume what others may be thinking of me. I, too, have an opinion of people when meeting them for the first time. Thoughts like, *"She's nice," "He's cute" or "He or she is funny looking,"* come to mind. So, I know it happens to other people when meeting me.

On one hand, I could honestly care less what most people think of me but on the other, I wonder if I'd care at all if I were smaller. I never try to overdo it, because you're either going to love me or not, but if I had to be honest, I care. I care how I represent my husband and I care how he represents me. I want him to be proud when I walk into a room.

Listen, I'm a woman and we all want to feel sexy, beautiful, and strong. I hate that I sometimes wrestle with these thoughts. It makes my stomach turn, literally. I want those foul thoughts dragged through the streets and left for dead, but they're here, and they aren't going anywhere until I face them.

I could lose 100 pounds today and still meet new people that are not impressed with me. I'd have enough of these thoughts! I'm sexy and I know it! Fat rolls, FUPA, double chin, and all. I had to be enough for me and saying it wasn't enough. I had to believe it. It doesn't matter what anyone thinks of me. I had to learn to truly value myself and the fat that came with me.

If I'm unhappy with my physical appearance, then it's up to me to change it. I am determined to leave this life loving every bit of me. No old mindset and new person's opinion is going to stop that.

You are the only one that can kill your thinking errors. You must challenge the bad thoughts, cut them at their roots, and render them powerless. You will either declare victory or defeat. If you want your relationship to prosper, then you will have to slay the "Fat Mindset" dragon. My marriage is worth the fight. I am worth the fight and I am determined that I am going to win.

Self-Reflection:

1. Are you a people pleaser?
2. Do you judge others based on their appearance?
3. Do you care what others think of you? Why or why not?
4. Are you affected by what others think of you?

Yes, He's in Love with a BTG Girl-Part 2

Confidence Restored

A couple's engagement photos went viral when the slimly built fiancé was captured holding his very full-figured bride-to-be. I guess his "bionic strength" wowed people. One lady wrote, "I'm out here killing myself in the gym, meanwhile fat girls are getting married!"

I'm confused. Is there some unspoken rule that says, "You must be a certain size to get married?" Is the marital union reserved for women whose thighs don't rub together, only? I laughed so hard at her hatred that my belly shook, literally. I then turned my big behind over and snuggled up with my slimly built husband.

The bible says, "Hope deferred makes the heart grow sad." Her hope had yet to come, and her heart did a poor job of hiding her bitterness. I never understood how hating on another woman would help you get a man.

Another man wrote that he loved his wife's big thick thighs. They hold him tight like a momma bear holds her baby cub during hibernation. Her grip is secure, comforting, and as warm as a Georgia summer. She's fluffy like cotton candy, and he absolutely loves sweets!

The truth is, there are a lot of men that love big women. I know that seems unbelievable, but it's our dope reality. I am the biggest woman my husband has ever dated. To assume that he loves big girls because he's with me is like assuming that every Corvette owner loves NASCAR. You can't generalize based on one isolated situation. I don't know if this kind of assumption gives women some sort of reassurance, but I assure you, this is only an illusion created by an insecure woman to feel safe. There is enough love out here for everyone. The sooner you realize that the better your life will be.

3 Types of Men:

- ***The 1st type of man is attracted to what he lacks.*** *If he's insecure in any way, he may date someone that builds his confidence in that area. Dating a beautiful woman, for example, may make him feel more secure about himself. He looks at her as an achievement. She's his trophy. He measures his value by her level of attraction. The hotter she is, the better he feels about himself.*

- ***The 2nd type of man is attracted to all women.*** *Their shape, size, and color doesn't matter to him. If she's a female, he's down. A warm body is what he constantly craves.*

- ***The 3rd type of man is attracted to confidence.*** *This manly man thinks confidence is a woman's sexiest attribute. If you love you, then so will he!*

You typically attract what you are. Don't hate on another woman for what she attracts. If you want something different, you must be the change you want to see. I never worried about meeting men because my confidence demanded attention. They didn't know that I had insecurities about my size because when I was on, I was on.

When I met my husband back in 2009, I was wearing a pair of size 18 whitewash jeans. You couldn't tell me that I wasn't all he'd prayed for. The cute face, thick waist, and genuine confidence that attracted him back then is what has his "nose open" to this day. Yes, I have insecurities, but I absolutely love myself and nothing can take that away from me anymore.

I couldn't rely on a flat stomach and a tiny waist. I had no choice but to unlock, unleash and unwrap my confidence for all to see. I was forced to be persistent in my pursuit of genuine happiness. It's been a long journey, but

I've made it.

Whether you were always a big girl or became one later in life, just know that you are not alone. There is a community of full-figured, fully-loved women. And if someone ever stares at you wondering how you got that sexy husband, you look them in the face with immense confidence and say, *"Yes honey, he's in love with a BIG girl!"*

Self-Reflection:

1. What type of man do you attract?

2. What are you looking for in a partner?

3. What makes you beautiful?

4. What makes you unique or special?

5. Have you always been confident? If not, why?

Notes

Fatherless Daughters: How Growing Up Without a Dad Affects Women – We Have Kids

https://wehavekids.com/family-relationships/When-Daddy-Dont-Love-Their-Daughters-What-Happens-to-Women-Whose-Fathers-Werent-There-for-Them

Does a Negative Body Image Affect Your Marriage? - Focus on the Family

https://www.focusonthefamily.com/marriage/does-a-negative-body-image-affect-your-marriage/

How to Stop Comparing Yourself to Others | RamseySolutions.com

https://www.ramseysolutions.com/personal-growth/how-to-stop-comparing-yourself-to-others

How a Life Coach Taught Me to Stop Comparing Myself to Others

https://www.healthline.com/health/mental-health/learned-stop-comparing

15 Things Most Moms Are Insecure About After Giving Birth

https://www.babygaga.com/15-things-most-moms-are-insecure-about-after-giving-birth/

This is why women gain weight after pregnancy - Times of India

https://timesofindia.indiatimes.com/life-style/parenting/pregnancy/why-women-gain-weight-after-pregnancy-decoded/articleshow/82288572.cms?

Is it Ever OK To Check Your Partner's Phone? Marriage Therapists Weigh In. | HuffPost Life

https://www.huffpost.com/entry/ok-to-check-partners-phone_n_5b6b68fbe4b0bdd0620628b1#:~:text=So%2C%20Is%20It%20Ever%20OK,like%20a%20jerk%20for%20snooping.

Made in United States
Orlando, FL
13 June 2023